THE THREE BROTHERS

A Serbian Folk Tale Retold by
MOLLIE CLARKE

Illustrated by William Stobbs

FOLLETT PUBLISHING COMPANY *Chicago New York*

Copyright © 1965 by Mollie Clarke. First published 1965 by Rupert Hart-Davis, London. Published 1967 in the United States of America by Follett Publishing Company, Chicago. All rights reserved. No part of this book may be reproduced in any form without written permission from the publisher. Printed in the United States of America.

Library of Congress Catalog Card Number: 67-20996   First Printing   T/L 8713

Once upon a time there were three
brothers. Their names were Peter and
Stevan and Marko. Marko was the
youngest brother.

The three brothers were very poor.

The three brothers lived in a hut by the edge of a wood.

Beside the hut grew the finest pear tree in the land.

The brothers were very proud of their pear tree and they took good care of it.

One day, the three brothers saw an
old woman sitting under the pear tree.

The old woman said, "I am hungry and
thirsty. Please give me one of your pears."

So Marko picked two of the finest
pears and gave them to the old woman.

The old woman ate one of the pears and put the other one carefully in her pocket.

She said, "You have been kind to an old woman and now I shall be kind to you. Come with me."

So Peter and Stevan and Marko followed the old woman through the wood.

Soon they came to a deep, wide river.
The old woman said to Peter, "Make a
wish and it shall be granted."

Peter looked at the deep, wide river.
He said, "I wish that all this water
could be changed into wine and that all
the wine belonged to me."

6

As soon as Peter had finished speaking,
the water changed into wine.

Men and barrels appeared on the river
bank and the men began filling the
barrels with wine.

"All this wine belongs to you," said
the old woman. "Stay here and you will
be rich."

Then Stevan and Marko followed the old
woman until they came to a field where
there were a great many doves.

The old woman said to Stevan, "Make a
wish and it shall be granted."

Stevan looked at the doves. He said,
"I wish that all the doves could be
changed into cows and that all the cows
belonged to me."

As soon as Stevan had finished
speaking, the doves changed into cows.

There were cowherds to look after the
cows and dairymaids to make butter and
cream.

The old woman said to Stevan, "All
these cows belong to you. Stay here
and you will be rich."

Then Marko followed the old woman until they came to the walls of a great city.

The old woman said to Marko, "Make a wish and it shall be granted."

"I wish to marry the wisest and most beautiful woman in the world," said Marko.

"Then you must marry the Tsar's daughter," said the old woman, "for she is the wisest and most beautiful woman in the world."

She took the pear out of her pocket and gave it to Marko. She said, "You must give this pear to the Tsar's daughter."

Then the old woman took Marko to the
palace and led him to the room where
the Tsar and his daughter were receiving
their guests.

A rich nobleman went up to the Tsar.
He said, "I wish to marry the Tsar's
daughter."

Then the rich nobleman gave the Tsar's
daughter a silver cloak embroidered with
pearls.

A fine prince went up to the Tsar.
He said, "I wish to marry the Tsar's
daughter."

Then the fine prince gave the Tsar's
daughter a casket filled with jewels.

Then Marko, in his ragged clothes, went up to the Tsar.

He said, "I am a poor man but I wish to marry the wisest and most beautiful woman in the world."

He gave the pear to the Tsar's daughter and said, "I have brought you a golden pear from the finest pear tree in the land."

The Tsar said, "Which of these men
should marry my daughter?"

The old woman said, "Let each man
plant a vine. If one of the vines
bears fruit by tomorrow morning, then
the man who planted that vine shall
marry the Tsar's daughter."

So the three men planted vines.

The next morning, the Tsar and his
daughter, the nobleman, the prince,
Marko and the old woman went to look at
the vines.

The vine which the nobleman had
planted had green leaves.

18

The vine which the prince had planted
was twice as tall as the nobleman's
vine and had flowers.

But the vine which Marko had planted was twenty times as tall as the prince's vine and it was covered with bunches of purple grapes.

The Tsar said, "The matter has been decided. The poor man must marry my daughter."

All the princes and noblemen in the
land came to the wedding of Marko and
the Tsar's daughter.

After the wedding, the old woman said
to Marko, "Your wish has been granted.
You have married the wisest and most
beautiful woman in the world. But now
you must take her back to your hut."

So Marko took the Tsar's daughter
back to his hut by the edge of the wood.

The old woman went away and forgot
about the three brothers.

But next year, when she saw pears
ripening on the pear trees, she remembered
Peter and Stevan and Marko.

She put on her ragged clothes and
set off to find them.

First she came to the meadow with cows
and cowherds and dairymaids.

A rich man came up to her and she saw
that it was Stevan.

She said, "I am very hungry. Please
give me a piece of cheese."

"No, I shall not," said Stevan. "I do
not give my cheese to beggars."

The old woman said, "Then you do not deserve your good fortune. I shall no longer grant your wish."

As soon as she had finished speaking, the cowherds and the dairymaids disappeared and the cows changed back into doves.

The old woman went on until she came to the river bank where men were filling barrels with wine.

A rich man came up to her and she saw that it was Peter.

She said, "I am very thirsty. Please give me some wine."

"No, I shall not," said Peter. "I do not give my wine to beggars."

26

The old woman said, "Then you do not
deserve your good fortune. I shall no
longer grant your wish."

As soon as she had finished speaking,
the men and the barrels disappeared
and the wine changed back to water.

27

At last the old woman came to the hut
and Marko and the Tsar's daughter ran out
to greet her.

She said, "I am hungry and thirsty.
Please give me something to eat and
drink."

Marko and the Tsar's daughter said,
"Come into the hut. We are very poor
but you shall share what we have."

Marko picked the finest pear on the
pear tree and gave it to the old woman.

The Tsar's daughter fetched a jug of
water and a small piece of stale bread.

But when they sat down to eat, the
small piece of stale bread became a
large, fresh loaf and when they drank
the water, they found that it was
wine.

When they had finished their meal, the
old woman said, "You have been kind to
me and I shall be kind to you."

As soon as she had finished speaking,
the hut changed into a beautiful palace
filled with everything that Marko and
the Tsar's daughter could wish for.

Presently, Peter and Stevan came back
to find their old hut. They were
astonished to find Marko and the Tsar's
daughter living in a beautiful palace.

When Marko heard what had happened
to his brothers, he said, "You may live
in the palace and share all we have
if you will do one thing."

"Tell us what it is," said the brothers,
"and we shall do it."

"You must look after the pear tree,"
said Marko, "for it is the finest pear
tree in the land and the cause of our
good fortune."